Napoleon

by L. DU GARDE PEACH, OBE MA PhD DLitt

with illustrations by JOHN KENNEY

Ladybird Books Loughborough

NAPOLEON BONAPARTE

Napoleon Bonaparte was one of the two greatest soldiers the world has ever known. The other was Alexander the Great, who died more than 2,000 years before Napoleon was born, and about whom you may read in another book in this series. As well as being a great general, Napoleon made many of the laws under which France is governed today.

Napoleon had more energy, more intelligence and a better brain than any other man in Europe. He was also able to work for twenty hours a day, with only four hours sleep.

All this, combined with his ability to decide instantly and correctly what to do either in a battle or a council chamber, enabled him, a poor boy from Corsica, to become Emperor of France and master of Europe at the age of thirty-five.

In 1768 the island of Corsica became part of France, and a year later Charles and Letizia Buonaparte had a son, their second, whom they christened Napoleoné. These names are Italian, because Corsica previously belonged to Italy. Napoleon later changed the spelling to the French form which we know today, and by which he will always be known to history.

Artillery
Officer

Gunner

Infantry
Sergeant

Trooper's
Sword

Musket

Scabbard

Bayonet

A Ladybird Book
Series 561

*Napoleon Bonaparte was one of the greatest
soldiers the world has known. He
conquered all western Europe, and might
have conquered Great Britain if it had
not been for Nelson and Wellington.*

This is his story.

We know very little about Napoleon's childhood. Corsica was a small island, and the Corsican people were mostly untaught peasants in revolt against their new French masters. Napoleon's father and, later, Napoleon himself were involved in a rebellion which failed. For a time they were obliged to leave the island.

Charles Buonaparte was related to a family which had belonged to the nobility of Tuscany, in Italy. A friend of the family, Count de Marboeuf, was able to help him to get a grant to send the young Napoleon to a military school at Brienne, in France.

He did not have a very happy time at school. He has been described as gloomy and not good at games. In addition, he spoke French with a strong Corsican accent, and was despised by the boys from rich French families because he was poor.

Napoleon was not a brilliant scholar. He was good at mathematics, and he liked history and geography. But he had a wonderful memory, and all his life he was always able to remember everything he read or heard. When it came to designing fortifications, or planning military exercises, he was far better than any of the other boys.

Because Napoleon was so good at mathematics he was sent to the artillery school in Paris, where his mathematics master reported that he was one of the most intelligent pupils he had ever had. In everything else, he failed to distinguish himself.

He was posted to the La Fère regiment of artillery as a sub-lieutenant, and this was the beginning of his wonderful career as the greatest military commander of his time.

Napoleon was now sixteen, and the year was 1785. In those days, cannon were nothing like the accurate long-range guns of today. They fired solid cannon balls, and also what was called grape-shot. This was like modern shrapnel, and consisted of a lot of small balls about the size of golf balls, which scattered and could therefore kill or wound a lot of people at one shot.

Although soldiers in those days wore wonderful uniforms, Sub-Lieutenant Bonaparte cannot have looked very distinguished. He was short, very thin and far from strong, and with a sallow complexion saved by handsome features and brilliant eyes.

Napoleon still thought of himself as a Corsican, rather than a Frenchman. But he was now a captain in the French army, and he was sent to put down a rising in Corsica led by a patriotic Corsican named Paoli. This meant a final break with Corsica, and Napoleon was obliged to remove his mother and her family to France.

Madame Bonaparte was a woman of strong character and determination. With her young children she managed to evade the followers of Paoli who tried to capture her.

The refugees had lost everything, and had only Napoleon's pay on which to live. But at this point his elder brother Joseph married the daughter of a rich merchant, somewhat against her father's wishes. If he had known that she would one day be the Queen of Spain, he might not have objected so strongly.

Napoleon wished to marry another daughter, but this time the father refused. When, only eleven years later, Napoleon became Emperor of France, he was probably sorry that he had turned down the young captain of artillery. This daughter later married one of Napoleon's generals, Bernadotte, and became Queen of Sweden. Bernadotte retained his throne, and his descendant is King of Sweden today.

The French Revolution had broken out in 1789, and France became a Republic three years later. The King had been murdered and the armies of all the European countries were gathering to avenge his death.

Some parts of France were still against the new Government. One of these was the port of Toulon, where the citizens had called in the assistance of some English warships. These were anchored in the harbour.

The French generals were unable to decide how to attack the town. They were not prepared to listen to the advice of a young captain of artillery. It was not until they were replaced by a general with more experience, that Napoleon was given the opportunity which changed his life, and was to affect all Europe.

Captain Bonaparte, by which name the future Emperor was then of course known, was put in command of the artillery. He had from the first insisted that the guns should be mounted on a promontory which commanded the harbour. This was now done, and Napoleon set up braziers to make the cannon balls red hot. When these started falling amongst them, the English ships left the harbour. Without their help, Toulon surrendered.

On the fall of Toulon, Napoleon was promoted to Brigadier. This was rapid promotion for a young man of only twenty-four. Many older soldiers were jealous of him, and many of the politicians distrusted him. But he was too useful an officer to be neglected.

Napoleon was next sent to the French army opposing the Austrians in northern Italy. The French generals were again incompetent, and when Napoleon arrived they at first refused to listen to him. When they did, there was an immediate change.

At the military school the young Napoleon had read a book on military tactics which he had never forgotten. It laid down the rules for anyone commanding an army: to choose a point of attack, and at that point to be stronger than the enemy, and secondly always to try to surprise the enemy by moving swiftly from one place to another.

By always remembering these two rules, Napoleon won one campaign after another, until it seemed he was invincible. Added to swiftness of movement, Napoleon possessed the ability to look at a map and at once to know how and where to move his soldiers to surprise the enemy.

Napoleon returned from Italy to find that his friends in the government had been replaced, and that he himself was out of favour. He was offered the command of some soldiers fighting against a part of France, the Vendée, which did not recognise the Revolutionary Government.

Napoleon refused, saying that he was an artilleryman and knew nothing about commanding infantry. This sounds strange coming from the man who was later to command hundreds of thousands of victorious infantrymen all over Europe.

It was at this point, in 1795, that the whole future, not only of Napoleon, but of a score of European countries including England, might have been changed. The Sultan of Turkey was asking for French artillery officers to help in organising his army. Napoleon was tempted, and applied for permission to go. It was refused.

Napoleon's fortunes seemed to be at a very low ebb. He was poor, out of favour, and often hungry. He even had to sell his watch to buy food. Then, as had happened before in his career, his luck changed overnight. His friend Barras, a politician but no soldier, found himself facing civil war in Paris. He sent for Napoleon, whom he remembered from the capture of Toulon.

The armed revolt, organised by the royalists, that is those who were in favour of a monarchy, was a serious one. They had 30,000 men ready to attack, and the Convention, which was the name of the French government, had only 8,000. But Napoleon Bonaparte was in command of them.

There was what we call a gun-park at a place named Sablons, and the royalists determined to capture it. They sent a battalion to seize the guns, but Napoleon got there first. He had no mercy. As soon as the royalists appeared, he opened fire with grape-shot and hundreds were killed. The rest ran away.

At other points in Paris, such as the famous Pont Royal, Napoleon dispersed the royalists, and by doing so earned the grateful thanks of the Convention. He was now well established, but he wanted again to prove himself where he knew he could do more, and do it better, than any other French general.

The war against Austria was not going well. Napoleon, who was now on friendly terms with the members of the Government, met and talked with the Minister who was in charge of military affairs. He applied to be sent to Italy to command the army.

The Minister for War, Carnot, agreed. General Bonaparte was to go to Italy in supreme command. But first something was to happen which later became of very great importance: his marriage.

As an out-of-work officer in disgrace, he had met Josephine de Beauharnais when he returned to her the sword of her husband, who had been killed in the French Revolution. She was six years older than Napoleon, and was at first scornful of the shabby young officer.

Barras was also a friend of Josephine de Beauharnais, and he assured her that the young General Bonaparte was very far from being as bad a match as he looked. Barras realised that here was a man not to be judged by the shabby coat and the lank straggling hair which we see in existing portraits of Napoleon at twenty-six.

Barras was far from knowing to what heights Napoleon would rise in less than ten years, but he said enough to make Josephine de Beauharnais believe that this was a man worth marrying. The marriage took place, and although, for reasons of state, Napoleon was later to divorce her, he never ceased to love her to the end of his life.

When General Bonaparte arrived in Italy, the older generals looked with disdain on the thin young man whom the politicians in Paris had put in command over them. They soon changed their minds.

Napoleon found the French army in very poor condition. Half the men were in rags and all were hungry; none had been paid for months. He began by promising to lead them to a land of plenty, where everything would be theirs to take. Honour, fame, and wealth were waiting if they had the courage to fight for it.

The words put new heart into the hungry soldiers. They saw that here was a man very different from the old generals who were content merely to let things drift.

Napoleon could be curt and masterful with his generals, but never with his soldiers. He went amongst them as a friend, remembered many of their names, and asked after their families. No general had ever done anything like this before, and they became devoted to him. His courage won their respect. In a battle at Lodi it was necessary to get command of a bridge. The Austrian bombardment was terrible but Napoleon brought up his guns and even loaded them himself.

The French soldiers, used to seeing their generals keep well out of danger, were amazed to see their new commander acting as a gunner. What was more, he knew exactly what to do and how to do it. After Lodi he was known throughout the army as 'le petit caporal'— the little corporal. The soldiers had adopted him as one of themselves: it was the highest honour of all.

Napoleon followed the tactics which were always his sure way to victory. He divided the enemy forces and, by swift marches, struck at their weakest points. Soon the Austrians were driven out of Italy and forced to make peace.

To gain a victory in Italy was important, but Napoleon knew that to the politicians in Paris, a victory was only important if it brought financial and other gains. He took care of his men, and he never forgot the politicians.

The French Treasury was almost empty. Napoleon made the beaten enemy pay more than sixty million francs which he sent back to France. This was to make him popular with the Government. So that the people of France should also have cause to thank him, he enriched their art galleries and museums with the loot of priceless treasures.

Napoleon had become the most famous man in France, but when he returned he knew that the politicians were not only jealous of his popularity, but were afraid of him. He realised, however, that the time had not yet come for him to overthrow them, and he kept himself very much in the background.

In the treaty with Austria, what is now Belgium had been given to France. This meant that the whole of the coast opposite Dover would be in French hands. The English Government, under the famous Prime Minister Pitt, could not agree to this and refused to recognise the treaty.

England was therefore still at war with France. The French Government decided to invade England, and sent Napoleon to Boulogne to report on the proposal. They thought it would also be a good way of getting him out of Paris.

Napoleon spent three weeks at Boulogne. He realised that the idea of invading England was quite impossible whilst the English fleet was in command of the Channel. He reported that the crossing would take seven or eight hours, and would only be possible during the hours of darkness. Preparations were, however, continued in order to deceive the English.

Meanwhile Napoleon had suggested another way of striking at England. He proposed to conquer Egypt and close the route to India. This would hit English trade with the East and would, he hoped, force England to ask for peace.

It was a dangerous operation. Nelson was in the Mediterranean with a fleet, and Napoleon well knew that the French ships were no match for the English fleet. In addition there would be unarmed ships carrying an army of 40,000 men. In spite of this, the French expedition sailed on May 19th, 1798, and landed safely in Egypt. Nelson had missed it by five miles in the darkest hour of a short May night.

Once ashore, Napoleon soon won a battle near the Great Pyramids and entered Cairo two months after landing. However, in August Nelson found the French fleet at anchor in Aboukir Bay and destroyed it. Napoleon and the French army were now cut off from France.

In other books in this series you can read all about Nelson and the destruction of the French fleet, also about the famous Rosetta stone, which Napoleon brought back with him when he managed to return to France, a year and a half later.

Napoleon was again fortunate. He sailed in a small frigate in October, 1799, and slipped through the English fleet unseen. He landed in France to be received everywhere as the man who would save the Republic.

There was good reason for this. All his conquests in Italy had been lost by incompetent generals, and there was disorder and discontent at home. The men who should have been governing the country were all plotting one against another. The royalists were hoping to restore the monarchy, and a German army was threatening invasion.

Once again Napoleon waited until the right moment. Then, with the aid of a famous Frenchman named Talleyrand, he dismissed the members of the Government. Within weeks Napoleon, with the title of First Consul, was master of France.

He used his new powers well, and much that he did remains to this day. He drew up a new code of laws known as the Code Napoleon, and he founded the Bank of France. Another thing which owes its beginning to Napoleon is the Order of the Legion of Honour, still today the highest honour to which a Frenchman can attain. Most of all, he restored order and good government.

The people of France were weary of war. They wanted peace, and they hoped that fear of Napoleon would prevent any country from attacking them. They were wrong. Pitt refused to make peace and, assisted with large sums of money from England, Austria again put an army in the field. Napoleon was forced to march against the Austrians.

Seven months after becoming First Consul, Napoleon led an army across the Great Saint Bernard pass. Thousands of men, horses, and mules had to struggle against terrible conditions. Napoleon wrote: "We are battling against ice, snow, gales, and avalanches." Encouraged by their indomitable general, who shared all their hardships, the army crossed the pass and came down on Italy, as Napoleon further wrote, "like a thunderbolt."

Napoleon never forgot he had been an artillery officer. Always he supported his attacks with heavy gunfire. The guns had all to be dismantled and dragged over the pass on wooden sledges by hundreds of men.

Napoleon determined to march on Milan, the capital of Northern Italy, but first he had to meet and destroy the Austrian army. The battle of Marengo was fought and won in June, one of the most difficult and hard-fought battles of Napoleon's career.

In the year 1800 Napoleon was thirty-one, and had already twice made the Austrian Emperor beg for peace. He returned to France more than ever the hero of the people, only to find that the politicians had been plotting against him. They had hoped that he would be killed in Italy. When he rode into Paris very much alive, they scattered and fled.

Peace with Austria was followed a year later by the Treaty of Amiens, signed by England. Neither side believed that it would last. The English fleet held the sea, but Napoleon was victorious on land. Neither trusted the other.

Nor did Napoleon trust the men whom he had forced to give up the government of France. He knew that when his term as First Consul came to an end, they would be fighting amongst themselves to succeed him. France might well be plunged into civil war.

There was only one thing to be done, and Napoleon did not hesitate. He had narrowly escaped assassination, supposedly by English agents, which roused the anger of the French people. They realised that without Napoleon the country would again be badly governed. On a poll of the whole population, 3,500,000 people voted Napoleon Bonaparte First Consul for life. It was the first step towards the Crown.

Napoleon became the Emperor of France on December 2nd, 1804. The ceremony was magnificent. The great church of Notre Dame in Paris glowed with colour. The splendid uniforms of the officers, and the gorgeous robes of Napoleon himself, had never before been equalled.

The Pope came to Paris to crown the new Emperor, but at the supreme moment of the ceremony, Napoleon took the crown from the hands of the Pope. None but Napoleon was fitted to crown Napoleon. By this he signified to the world that he owed the crown to his own efforts, and to none other.

An Emperor needs a Court, but all the nobles of the Court of Louis XVI had been executed or driven out of France. Napoleon created a new nobility by making his friends and relatives into princes and dukes, counts and barons. Talleyrand, who had helped him to become First Consul, was created Prince of Benevento.

At the age of thirty-four the poor boy, mocked for his shabby clothes and his Corsican accent at the school at Brienne, had become an Emperor. As she watched the gorgeous ceremony of the crowning of her son, Napoleon's mother shook her head and murmured, "If only it lasts."

Napoleon Bonaparte had reached the height of his ambition. He could go no further. He had achieved an Imperial Crown, but he knew that only by making himself master of Europe could he continue to be master of France.

The French people rejoiced in the well-ordered government and the new prosperity. Only Napoleon realised the dangers ahead. Behind the scenes, commanding the sea and pouring money into the rapidly arming countries of Europe, was England. He determined, first of all, to invade and crush the enemy he feared most.

For two years, small boats had been assembled in French harbours facing the English coast, and an army was encamped near Boulogne ready to be transported to England. In England an army was armed and ready, but the chief defence depended on the navy. Unless Napoleon could command the Channel, any attempt to bring thousands of men across it would be doomed to disaster.

The French fleet tried to lure the English ships away, but always some remained in the narrow seas. At last the two fleets met at Trafalgar. The combined French and Spanish fleet was destroyed by Nelson, and Napoleon knew that his dream of conquering England was at an end.

Napoleon was no sailor and never understood sea warfare. Everywhere the English ships interfered with his plans. "Wherever wood can float," he cried angrily, "there you will find the English!" Fortunately for us, he was right.

Even before the defeat at Trafalgar, the soldiers encamped at Boulogne were needed elsewhere. Austria, Prussia, and Russia were all threatening war with France. Napoleon decided to act first. Marching across Europe with a speed which seemed impossible to his enemies, he defeated the Austrians, the Prussians, and the Russians in a series of battles which astounded the world. England alone remained unconquered.

Napoleon, unable to fight on land with England, attempted to ruin her trade. He tried to make all the nations of Europe promise not to buy anything from, or sell anything to, the English merchants.

They all reluctantly agreed, and at a meeting with the Czar of Russia on a raft in the middle of the River Niemen, the agreement was confirmed. It was a strange meeting. The two Emperors, Alexander I of Russia and Napoleon I of France met with every show of friendship, but neither trusted the other. It was not long before Alexander broke all his promises to Napoleon.

We must remember that all this time Napoleon was one man trying to govern all Europe. It was too great a task. Every country except France hated him and longed for revenge. His military genius had conquered them, but he could not be everywhere. When he left things to others, battles were lost and conquered peoples broke out in rebellion.

More and more countries were secretly trading with England, and Napoleon had to send troops to many ports in an attempt to stop the English ships which sailed openly into continental harbours.

Napoleon had awarded the Spanish throne to his brother Joseph, and Spain was the first country openly to rebel against him. The Spaniards refused to accept Joseph, and Napoleon was obliged to cross the Pyrenees himself to retrieve the disasters suffered by his generals. Whilst he was in Spain, Austria again declared war.

Making another amazing dash across Europe, at a time when the pace of a horse was the fastest at which a man could travel, Napoleon met and again beat the Austrians at the battle of Wagram. This time he determined to make sure of Austria. Divorcing Josephine, he forced the Austrian Emperor to give him his daughter Marie Louise in marriage.

At forty-one the Corsican boy had married the daughter of the proudest Royal House in Europe. At last he felt himself the equal of the monarchs over whom he had been victorious in war, but who had sneered at him as a Corsican adventurer.

The monarchs thought differently, and his friend of Tilsit, Alexander of Russia, justified all Napoleon's suspicions by turning against him. Although he knew the difficulty of fighting a war in Russia, Napoleon had already beaten the Russians once at Friedland, and had no doubt that he could beat them again.

He assembled the largest army which had ever been gathered together and marched into Russia. Expecting soon to find a Russian army opposing him, Napoleon found only a countryside swept bare, with villages and even towns burnt before him. A battle at Borodino was won, but still the Russians retreated.

At last Moscow was reached, with only the annoyance of a few skirmishes with Cossacks—Russian cavalry. Now, thought Napoleon, the Russians must sue for peace. Next morning he awoke to find Moscow in flames from end to end. Napoleon waited a month. The Russians gave no sign. It was late in October: winter was at hand. Napoleon had no option but to retreat.

The retreat from Moscow was one of the most terrible military disasters in history. More than a thousand miles from the nearest point of France, the army had to march over roads lost under snowdrifts, through howling blizzards, with the thermometer seventy degrees below freezing. Few of those who had crossed the river Niemen into Russia in June ever got back to France.

Napoleon left the army and made a non-stop journey to Paris, mostly in a sleigh behind relays of horses galloping through the night over the frozen snow. Once in France he called up a new army. But the nations of Europe, encouraged by his defeat in Russia, were all against him. He beat them in battle after battle, but he was gradually driven back on Paris itself.

The end came when, in March, 1814, he ceased to be Emperor of France. It seemed that the amazing career of the boy from Corsica was finished. He was forty-five and still the greatest general in Europe, but the empire which he had built up had collapsed. Napoleon Bonaparte was finished. So thought the rulers of Austria, Germany, Russia, and England, as they watched the ship which carried Napoleon to exile on the island of Elba, fade into the mist.

Napoleon remained on Elba less than a year. Louis XVIII was on the throne of France, and everywhere disbanded soldiers were wishing that ' the little corporal ' would come back and lead them to fresh victories. Then, suddenly and unexpectedly, he came.

As he travelled across France, people thronged the streets to cheer him. An army was sent from Paris to capture him. When it approached, he walked forward alone to meet it. Suddenly, at the sight of their hero of a hundred battles, the soldiers were all shouting, "Vive l'Empereur!" He marched into Paris at the head of the troops sent to arrest him. Louis XVIII ran for his life.

The nations of Europe, including Britain, had been disbanding their armies, thinking that Napoleon was safe on the island of Elba. Napoleon's only hope was to crush such forces as remained under arms, before the disbanded soldiers could be remobilised.

Napoleon quickly raised an army of veterans. He knew that there were two armies in the field against him, but they were fifteen miles apart. Wellington was at Quatre Bras, about ten miles south of Brussels and Blücher, with a Prussian army, was fifteen miles to the south-east, at the village of Ligny. Napoleon decided to attack each of them before they could unite.

Napoleon was unwell, and his generals made many mistakes. Although Wellington was forced to retreat from Quatre Bras, and Blücher was driven out of Ligny, neither victory was followed up as it should have been. What was more disastrous for Napoleon was that he believed Blücher to be retreating away from Wellington, whereas actually he was marching north to join him.

The English took up a position near the village of Waterloo, a few miles south of Brussels: unknown to Napoleon, Blücher was near Wavre, seven or eight miles to the east. The battle of Waterloo started by attempts to take some farmhouses which were in front of the English position. This failed, and Napoleon attacked Wellington's position with cavalry and infantry. The English formed squares of bristling bayonets against which the French charged again and again. They were unable to break them.

It was towards evening when the Prussians reached the battlefield. Their arrival made victory certain.

Napoleon surrendered and spent the rest of his life on the lonely island of St. Helena in the South Atlantic, far away from France, guarded by English soldiers, and with English ships patrolling the surrounding seas. He was too dangerous and too great a man to be free.

British ships
in control of the
seas

London

Boulogne

Paris

Waterloo

Brienne

Napoleon
at school

Crossing the Alps

St. Bernards Pass

Toulon

Elba

Corsica
(Napoleon
birth pla

Invasion
of
Spain

French fleet
defeated at
Trafalgar

British ships
being driven off

NAPOLEON'S CAMPAIGNS IN EUROPE & EGYPT